Mood Pocket Mud Bucket

Deborah Turney Zagwyn

Fitzhenry & Whiteside

Mood Pocket, Mud Bucket

Fitzhenry & Whiteside
195 Allstate Parkway
Markham, Ontario L3R 4T8

Design: Ian Gillen
Typesetting: ISIS Communications

Canadian Cataloguing in Publication Data
Zagwyn, Deborah Turney
  Mood pocket, mud bucket
ISBN 0-88902-426-X
I. Title.
PS8599.A48M66 1988   jC813'.54   C88-093662-2
PZ7.Z33Mo 1988

For Les
who knows his Mud Bucket inside and out.
For Millie
who knows her Cow, from hoof to snout.
For Leo, my husband
who builds my working spaces
and
For Sonia, my daughter
with the wonderful faces.

Sonia had wild red hair that stuck up in two tufts, one above each ear, and these served as latches to hook her faces onto.

Sonia's faces were never masklike. They never hid the way she felt inside. She kept them in her pocket when she wasn't wearing them — faces for every mood and occasion — rainy mornings or sunny afternoons, sad beginnings or happy endings.

Some of her faces looked like the faces in the family photo album.

"You have your mother's smile and your gramma's frown," relatives would say, "and your father's forehead and your grampa's nose."

Often, after the relatives had gone home, Laslo (Sonia's older friend) would stop by for a late cup of tea. Sonia would be climbing into bed when she'd hear him stamping his feet on the porch below.

"I'm as parched as a set of lizard's lips!" he'd announce.

And while her mom put the kettle on he'd stomp up the stairs and pop his head in her doorway.

"Don't you worry about what yer relateds say, Sonia. You look more like yerself every day."

One stormy, spring morning as the wind whistled in the eaves and the robins in the cottonwood tree were wishing they had umbrellas, Sonia woke up feeling moodier than usual. She could hear her parents grumbling downstairs, and smell the wet wood smoking in the cookstove.

After frowning at herself in the mirror, Sonia put on her kangaroo smock with the big pocket and slipped her sleepy face back into her nightie. Her slippers had lost themselves, so she padded down the stairs in bare feet.

Down in the kitchen her parents looked worried. Sonia searched her smock pocket for a worried face too.

"The cows have broken through the fence. The lower field is flooded and the lake is lapping up against the barn," her mother said. "The chickens are wearing hipwaders. Your dad's going up to Laslo's place to get help."

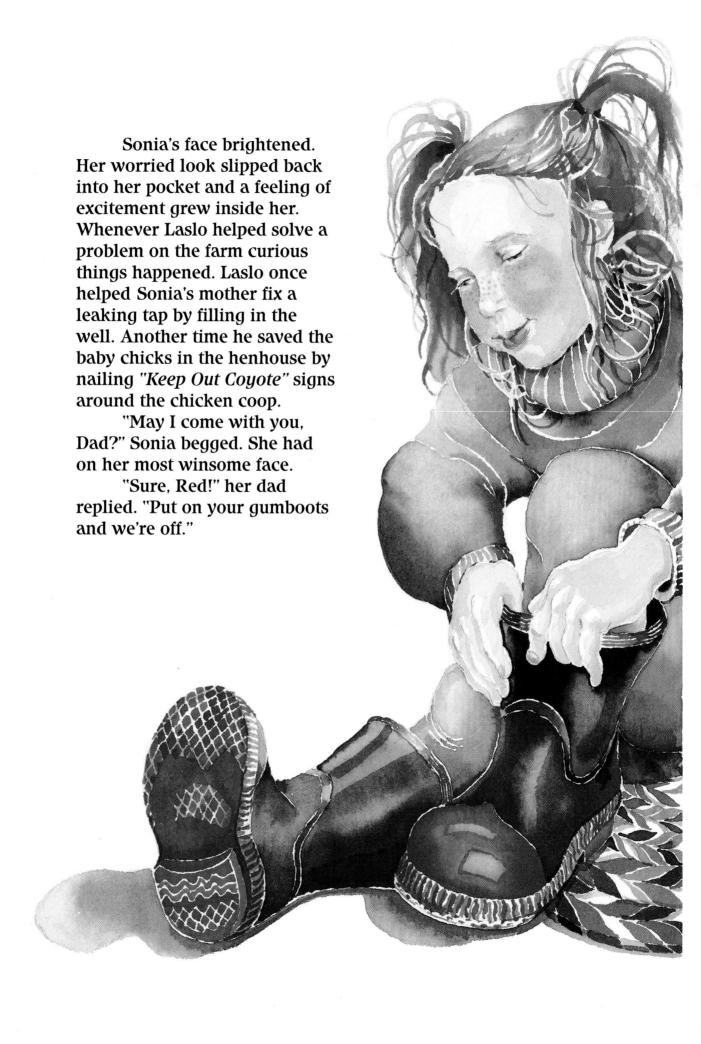

Sonia's face brightened. Her worried look slipped back into her pocket and a feeling of excitement grew inside her. Whenever Laslo helped solve a problem on the farm curious things happened. Laslo once helped Sonia's mother fix a leaking tap by filling in the well. Another time he saved the baby chicks in the henhouse by nailing *"Keep Out Coyote"* signs around the chicken coop.

"May I come with you, Dad?" Sonia begged. She had on her most winsome face.

"Sure, Red!" her dad replied. "Put on your gumboots and we're off."

The sun was just breaking through the clouds as Sonia and her dad drove through Laslo's gate, past his used T.V. collection, past his used grader blade collection, his used rubber tire collection, and past the jumble of used fridges.

Finally they stopped at Laslo's garage.

Laslo was sitting inside, using his backhoe bucket for a chair, reading a week-old newspaper and smoking his pipe. The fan on Laslo's wood heater was making a whirring sound, and underneath a tabby cat was cleaning its whiskers. The room was a clutter of nuts and bolts and grease. It was a friendly place.

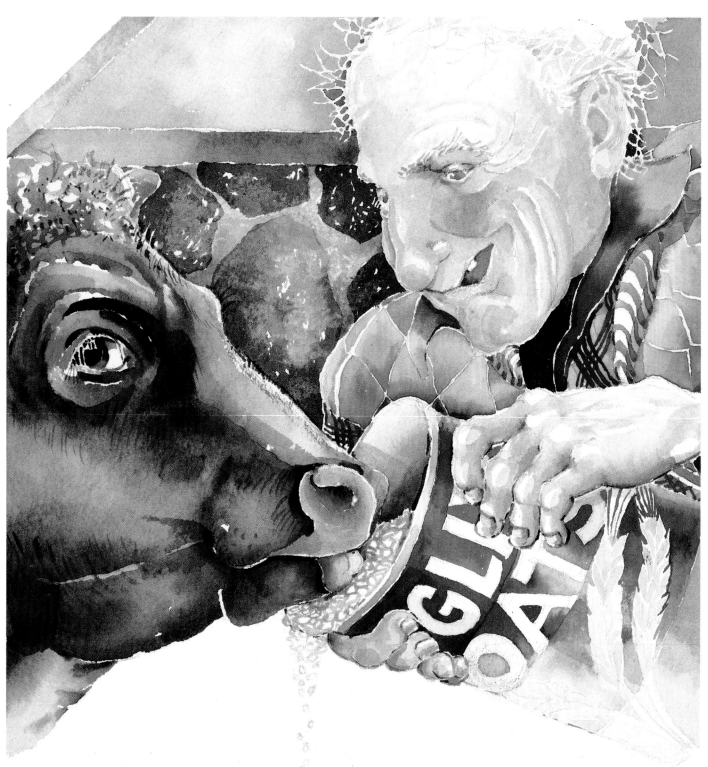

"Hello Laslo," said Sonia's dad.

"We need your help. Have you seen our six cows?"

"Yup!" Laslo replied "I've got them corralled in my basement. They told me your barn was floating and they didn't care for wet hay. I gave them some Oglivie oatmeal and played the phonograph for them."

Sonia's face was grinning from ear to ear. Laslo had the cows in his basement, with his three wringer-washing-machines and his broken sump pump. That must be a funny sight.

"You're kidding, Laslo!" Sonia's dad chuckled. "Let's get those cows down to the upper pasture before they tear your basement apart! I don't suppose you could lend us a hand fixing the dike on the lake side of the barn?"

Laslo stroked his backhoe bucket and knocked his pipe against its side.

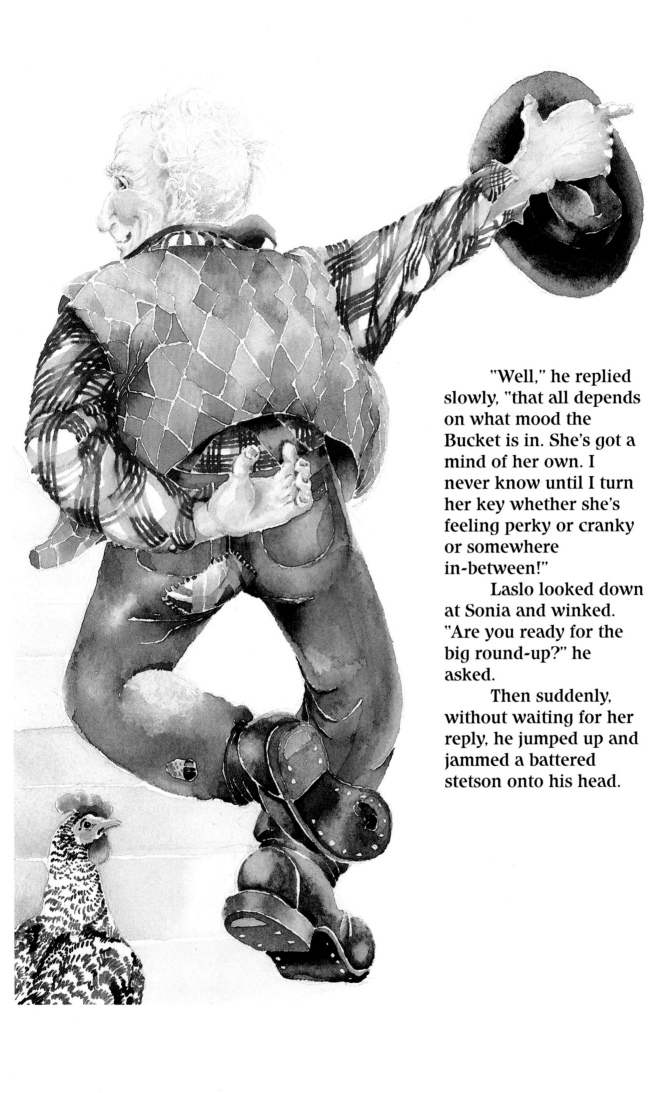

"Well," he replied slowly, "that all depends on what mood the Bucket is in. She's got a mind of her own. I never know until I turn her key whether she's feeling perky or cranky or somewhere in-between!"

Laslo looked down at Sonia and winked. "Are you ready for the big round-up?" he asked.

Then suddenly, without waiting for her reply, he jumped up and jammed a battered stetson onto his head.

The Bucket didn't even hesitate
when Laslo turned her key. She started
right away, rumbling contentedly while
Sonia's dad opened the garage doors. She
looked and sounded like a big purring
yellow cat.

Sonia trotted behind the men
to the basement of Laslo's house,
where they let the cows out —
all six of them.

Laslo's cellar was a mess. His wringer-washing-machines were standing in cowflops.

"Let's round up them doggies," Laslo whooped, and, swinging Sonia onto his shoulders, he marched over to where the Bucket was still idling by the garage. On the way he paused to pull down his washline and loop it into a lasso. Then, climbing onto the leather backhoe seat, which looked a lot like a saddle, Laslo plopped Sonia onto his lap. Sonia's dad nodded goodbye as Laslo put the Bucket in gear.

Puff, Puff, Puff it went like a dragon, and *Chug, Chug, Chug* like a train. Sonia's smiling face turned to a frightened face. Then Laslo tweaked her nose and yelled over the sound of the machine that she was the cowgirl for him. And, in an instant Sonia knew they'd embarked upon the biggest adventure of all.

Laslo's mud bucket moved into position behind the cows and sent them scurrying down the driveway toward the hayfield. The cows rolled their eyes and kicked up their heels. The backhoe honked her horn, revved her motor, and rocked her bucket. Laslo laughed and waved his hat in the air.

"Yahoo!" he shouted. "Hoof it!" And they rode across the ditch and out into the meadow.

The Bucket zig-zagged behind the bellowing herd and forced them through the upper pasture gate. Laslo was whooping and hollering and Sonia was honking the horn at the rear. It was a wild victory.

As soon as the cows were safely back in the pasture Laslo and Sonia scooped up buckets full of earth and dumped them onto the soggy dike. Finally the lake had no choice but to stay where it belonged. The stampeding cows turned into sleepy cud-chewers, and the white-capped waves of the lake were now rolling gently in to the shore.

Sonia and Laslo left the barn steaming in the afternoon sunlight and bounced the backhoe past the old crabapple orchard to Sonia's house. Outside on the doorstep a robin was sunbathing in the dog dish.

Inside, Sonia's mother was no longer worried. She was singing to the radio and putting teacups on the table.

"Thanks, Laslo," she said, wiping the mud off Sonia's cheek with her apron. Then she knelt down and whispered, "That's quite a tired-but-happy face you have there, Sonia!"

Sonia smiled and gave her a hug.

Laslo settled himself in the old stuffed rocker by the table and filled up his pipe. Sonia nestled next to him and looked for her favourite tattoo on his arm. It was a crimson sailor wrestling with a blue sea-serpent.

"Did the sailor win, Laslo?" She already knew the answer but she had to ask him one more time.

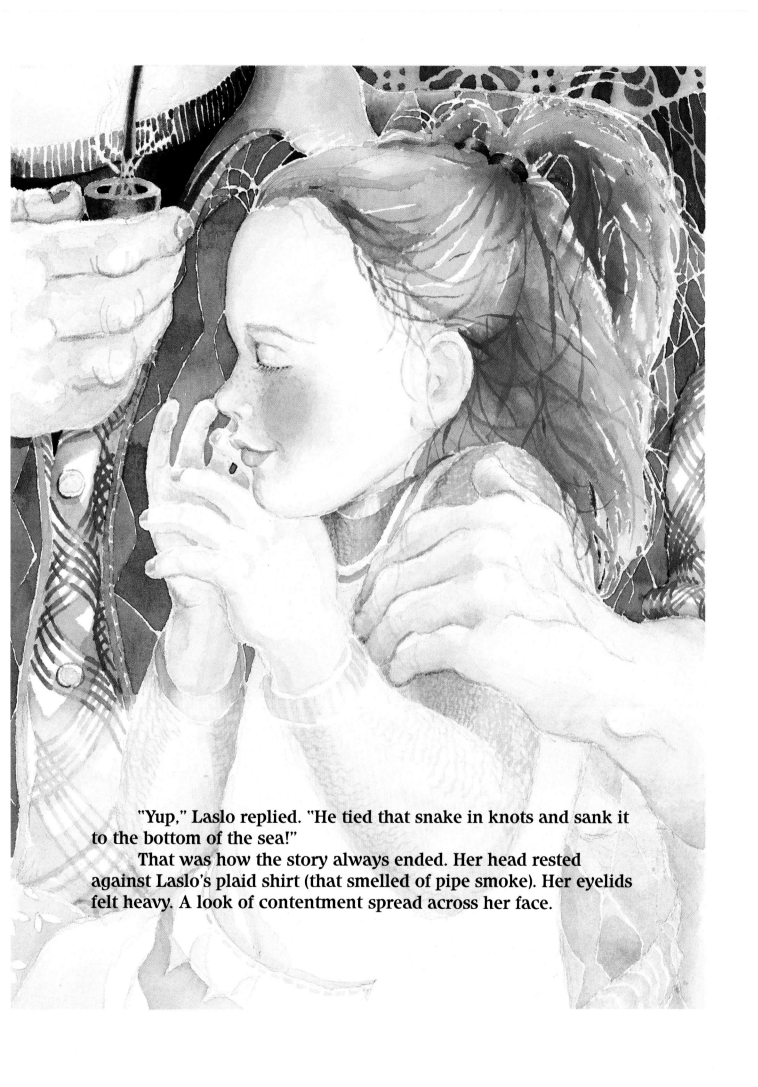

"Yup," Laslo replied. "He tied that snake in knots and sank it to the bottom of the sea!"

That was how the story always ended. Her head rested against Laslo's plaid shirt (that smelled of pipe smoke). Her eyelids felt heavy. A look of contentment spread across her face.

Printed and bound in Hong Kong